A Beginning-to-Read Book

Dear Dragon Eats Out

by Margaret Hillert
Illustrated by David Schimmell

NORWOOD HOUSE PRESS

The **Dear Dragon** series is comprised of carefully written books that extend the collection of classic readers you may remember from your own childhood. Each book features text focused on common sight words. Through the use of controlled text, these books provide young children with abundant practice recognizing the words that appear most frequently in written text. Rapid recognition of high-frequency words is one of the keys for developing automaticity which, in turn, promotes accuracy and rate necessary for fluent reading. The many additional details in the pictures enhance the story and offer opportunities for students to expand oral language and develop comprehension.

Shannon Cannon

Shannon K. Cannon, Ph.D.
Literacy Consultant

Norwood House Press • P.O. Box 316598 • Chicago, Illinois 60631
For more information about Norwood House Press please visit our website at
www.norwoodhousepress.com or call 866-565-2900.

Paperback ISBN: 978-1-60357-637-6

The Library of Congress has cataloged the original hardcover edition with the following call number: 2013029769

This paperback edition was published in 2015.

287R—102015
Printed in ShenZhen, Guangdong, China.

Get up. Get up. Get ready.
Today we are going out to eat.

OK, I will get ready.
I will do this.

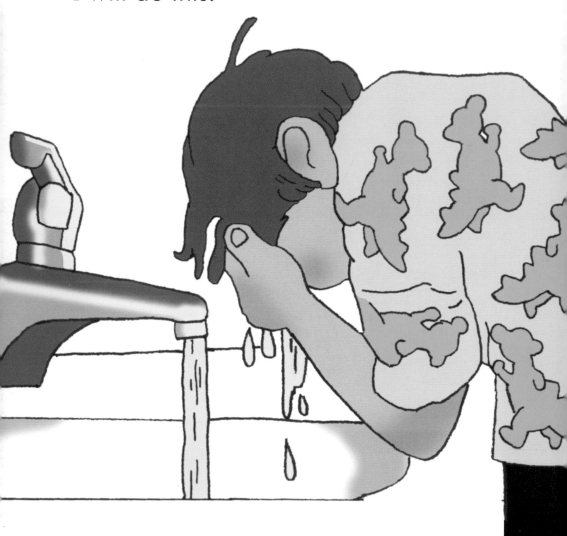

And I will do this.

Here I am Mother.
How do I look?

You look good.
Now let's go!

Come in. Come in.
I have a good spot for you.

Sit down.
Sit down.

Let me help, Mother.
I can do this.

No, No.
I am too big.

Let me sit here.
You sit there.

Put this on.

You will need it.

BREAKFAST MENU

CEREAL $1.50

JUICE $1.50

OATMEAL $1.50

EGGS AND BACON $3.50

PANCAKES $3.00

MUFFINS $3.50

We have to pick things out to eat.

Oh, boy.
Can I have what I want?

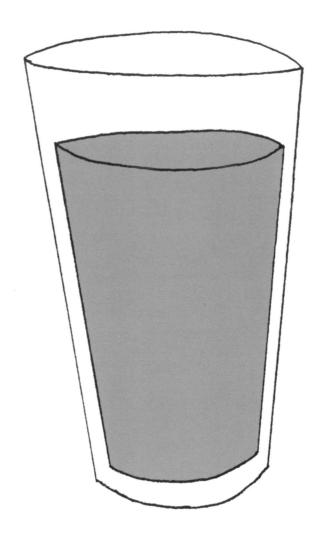

I like orange juice.

I like bacon and eggs.

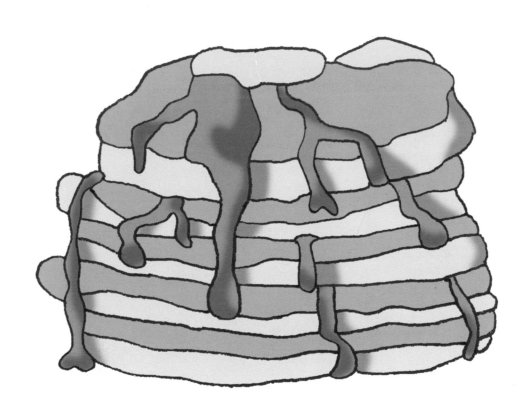

But, I think I'll have these.

Mother, what are you going to eat?

Mother will have eggs.
Dragon and I will have pancakes!

Here it comes.
Here comes something to eat.

Oh, Boy.
This is good.

I am here with you.
And you are here with me.
It is fun to eat out, Dear Dragon!

29

WORD LIST

***Dear Dragon Eats Out* uses the 68 words listed below.**

The **5** words bolded below serve as an introduction to new vocabulary, while the other 63 are pre-primer. You may wish to write the words on index cards and use them to help your child build automatic word recognition. Regular practice with these words will enhance your child's fluency in reading connected text.

a	for	let	**pancakes**	up
am	fun	let's	pick	
and		like	put	want
are	get	look		we
	go		ready	what
bacon	going	me		will
big	good	Mother	sit	with
boy			something	
but	have	need	spot	you
	help	no		
can	here	now	there	
come (s)	how		these	
		oh	things	
dear	I	ok	think	
do	I'll	on	this	
down	in	**orange**	to	
Dragon	is	out	today	
	it		too	
eat				
eggs	**juice**			

ABOUT THE AUTHOR   Margaret Hillert has written over 80 books for children who are just learning to read. Her books have been translated into many different languages and over a million children throughout the world have read her books. She first started writing poetry as a child and has continued to write for children and adults throughout her life. A first grade teacher for 34 years, Margaret is now retired from teaching and lives in Michigan where she likes to write, take walks in the morning, and care for her three cats.

Photograph by Glenna Washburn

ABOUT THE ADVISOR   Dr. Shannon Cannon is a teacher educator, in the School of Education at UC Davis where she also earned her Ph.D. in Language, Literacy, and Culture. Currently, she serves on the clinical faculty supervising pre-service teachers and teaching elementary methods courses in reading, effective teaching, and teacher action research. Her own research interests include; early literacy, research-based reading instruction, English learners, culturally responsive teaching, "funds of knowledge" perspectives, neuroscience, social emotional learning, and project-based learning. Shannon began her career in education teaching elementary-aged children in a year-round school. Subsequently, she spent over 15 years in educational publishing developing and writing curricular programs and providing professional development support to classroom teachers across the country.

ABOUT THE ILLUSTRATOR   David Schimmell served as a professional firefighter for 23 years before hanging up his boots and helmet to devote himself to working as an illustrator of children's books. David has happily created illustrations for the New Dear Dragon books as well as the artwork for educational and retail book projects. Born and raised in Evansville, Indiana, he lives there today with his wife and family.